# HOW TO TANKIE

The Anti-Imperialist's Guide

to the Modern World

CW01335800

# Contents

CONTENTS ............................................................1

INTRODUCTION .....................................................5

CHAPTER 1. RUSSIA IS JUST DEFENDING ITSELF. ...................7

CHAPTER 2. RUSSIA NEVER INVADED ANYONE. EVER...........9

CHAPTER 3. WHAT ABOUT IRAQ? ......................................14

CHAPTER 4. THE "NEAR ABROAD".......................................16

CHAPTER 5. PROTESTS IN THE "NEAR ABROAD"................18

CHAPTER 6. NATO EXPANSION...........................................21

CHAPTER 7. THE WARSAW PACT. ......................................25

CHAPTER 8. RESPECTING RUSSIA. .....................................27

CHAPTER 9. THREATENING TO DEFEND YOURSELF. ............29

CHAPTER 10. SEPTEMBER 1939 TO JUNE 1941. .................31

CHAPTER 11. WE JUST DON'T WANT A WAR YOU NEOCON
SHILL! ...........................................................................34

CHAPTER 12. THE PAST CHANGES QUICKLY. .......................39

CHAPTER 13. THE LAMESTREAM MEDIA. ...........................41

CHAPTER 14. IN UKRAINE, RUSSIA IS ONLY DOING WHAT
GREAT POWERS DO. ......................................................43

CHAPTER 15. EVERYONE WANTS TO OVERTHROW THE
KREMLIN.........................................................................46

CHAPTER 16. RUSSIA IS CONCERNED BY THE RISE OF THE
FAR RIGHT IN THE WEST. .................................................48

CHAPTER 17. THE SUCCESSOR STATE TO THE USSR. EXCEPT WHEN IT ISN'T. ..................................................................50

CHAPTER 18. CONCLUSION .................................................52

CHAPTER 19. QUIZ ANSWERS. ...........................................53

CHAPTER 21 WHAT LEVEL OF TANKIE ARE YOU? .................56

AUTHOR'S NOTE .................................................................58

## About the Author

Darth Putin (@DarthPutinKGB) is a semi-holographic, superior being created from a collection of body parts left over from Stalin's purges to form a 6'8" (that's 2 measurements) chiseled slab of a man that can tame Siberian tigers, wrestle bears to submission and impregnate women with a single glance.  He exists in a cryogenic, ageless state within a secret, hollowed-out mountain lair. There he practices denials and master strategy to innovate superior methods of converting anti-imperialists into superior tankies, the better to remorselessly counter the forces of colonialism.

This might be considered a work of satire.  Any relation
to any person, living or dead is purely unintentional.
Any facts in this book were placed there accidentally.

# Introduction

## Definition – What is a "tankie"?

Do you find yourself surrounded by imperialists who say Putin is a bad guy? Have you ever wondered why so many suddenly think Russia has invaded Ukraine and also mention all the other times Russia invaded someone? Do you find yourself thinking "but what about Iraq and WMD?" Are you called a "tankie", have no idea what it means but suspect it might be an insult? Fear not my fellow anti-imperialist, this book is for you!

What is a Tankie? A tankie used to be someone who followed the official Communist Party line in all things, most particularly when the Kremlin sent in the tanks: hence "tankie". Imperialists who think that autocrats from around the world should be held to the same standard as western leaders call you a "tankie" just because you don't think a Russian tank where it isn't invited is as bad as an American one also where it isn't welcome. They think it is an insult, but no! Wear the name with pride! You are on the right side of history and this book will tell you why - saving you the trouble of having to think about it yourself. Better still, it will teach you how to defeat imperialist facts in any and all debates!

So how do you be a good tankie? How do you properly, loyally fight the forces of imperialism and colonialism? Read on, dear comrade and find out!

## How to use this book

This book will dissect many common and predictable imperialist arguments and, at no extra cost, provide the official position that you, as a tankie should take. You may find that reality and logic are at odds with tenets of tankie-ism. But, as you will learn, reality has an imperialist bias and logic is a Western construct that can be disregarded.

Many chapters and topics covered connect to other facets of anti-imperialism, starting from the high-level position that "Russia is just defending itself" and "Russia has never invaded any country in history" before moving on to the less obvious, but no less important, topic of why logic is an imperialist construct that doesn't apply to you.

At the end of each section there is a short quiz to ascertain if you are an imperialist, colonialist warmonger or, hopefully, near the level of a professor of language who will one day explain why NATO is in fact unpopular. Enjoy and happy tankie-ing!

# Chapter 1.
# Russia is just defending itself.

In this current confrontation it is vital you, the tankie, understand that Russia is the victim. It is simply defending itself against an aggressive West. As the Kremlin (who is always truthful) frequently states: the West seeks three things. Firstly, to contain Russia, presumably within its own borders. The idea that Russia should be contained within Russia is as ludicrous as it is imperialist. Secondly, the West seeks to break Russia apart. This is because Russia is too rich in natural resources. Thirdly, jealousy. The fact that Russia can make its own "sovereign decisions", for itself and also for other countries too, makes the West jealous.

We shall expand upon these issues and others. For now, the key thing to understand is this: the West is engaged in a plot to break Russia into several mutually loathing, nuclear armed states each run by a madman. They wish to do this out of jealousy, as has been said, and also to rob Russia of her natural resources which the West either already has, can get from someone else, or will soon no longer need, but also for the massive benefit of catastrophic instability along Europe's borders and the subsequent flood of refugees.

Seen in this light, Russia's defensive policy to the hostile West makes perfect sense.

Thus, it is undeniable: all opposition to the Kremlin in Russia is either in league with, or a direct proxy of, the West and its desire to destroy Russia. We will discuss in detail in a later chapter how it is that Russians are incapable of protesting against any corrupt leaders themselves. For this chapter, all the tankies need to know is that they are.

Chapter 1: Quiz

1. The West is jealous of Russia's sovereignty over itself *and* of other countries. True/False
2. Should Russia be contained within Russia?
3. All opposition to the Kremlin is a CIA plot. True/False

# Chapter 2.
## Russia never invaded anyone. Ever.

Having established that Russia is defending itself from the perfidious West, we can now add some other foundations to being a good tankie. Only the West does bad things. Only the West is imperialist. Only the West invades countries for made-up reasons. Russia has never invaded any country in history.

The Russian Federation as it exists today was birthed onto the world as the planet's largest country as an act of God. On those occasions when the Russian military has entered other countries it has been a "Special Military Operation", or they have "been invited in by the legitimate authorities". There are other, legitimate, tankie reasons for Russian soldiers to be in another country that we will discuss later, but it has never been an invasion.

This a foundational rule in "How to Tankie". Russia, as an anti-imperialist, anti-colonial country, has never invaded anyone. Those times when an imperialist asks about Finland or Poland or Estonia or Lithuania or Latvia or Georgia or Ukraine can usually be dealt with by asking "what about Iraq?".

## Defending Russia in another country

Russia's neighbors frequently attack Russia. They often do this just as Russia's army is massed peacefully on their border in attack formation, forcing Russia to defend itself *en masse* in that neighboring country.

A famous version of this was in 1939 when Finland shelled the Soviet Union to start its war with the USSR. Finland, whose existence was a threat to the USSR despite being over 66 times smaller than the Soviet Union, decided to attack.  Russia/Soviet Union once again was forced to defend itself.  Similar examples will be discussed when we review how absolutely nothing happened before 1941 as well as more recently examples.

The fact that Yeltsin admitted and condemned the USSR's wrongs against Finland, and also other buffer states during the period when nothing happened, does not matter.  We will discuss this more later, but for now: What about Iraq?

## A country that recently ceased to exist

So impressive is the Russian military that it once entered a country that had abruptly ceased to exist. Imperialists call this "invading Poland", but, as we will learn, this had nothing to do with the treaty we were forced to sign with Nazi Germany.  Rather, the Soviet Union entered not-Poland in order to honor her humanitarian obligation to restore order and protect not-Poland's not-citizens. True, there was some incidental mass murder but even a child knows that one cannot liberate a people from fascism if you can't kill them.

## Assist the Legitimate Government

This is a favorite. You can't invade a country if it doesn't exist, but what do you do if it isn't being invaded by the Nazis at the same time and the current government won't invite you? Create a new government and have that one invite you in. This is why Russia never invaded Finland and, most recently, has not invaded Moldova, Georgia, or Ukraine because Russia has been "invited in" by the "legitimate government" the Kremlin had no role in creating at all.

Considering events following Euromaidan in 2014, Russia, which has absolutely nothing to do with the Lugansk and Donetsk People's Republics in the former Ukraine, has been invited in to assist those legitimate governments in defending themselves from so-called Ukraine. Who can explain why these rebels on Russia's border, who have nothing to do with Russia, and who want to join Russia, never run out of Russian weapons, Russian ammunition, Russian fuel, Russian parts, Russian soldiers, and Russian propaganda? Russia clearly has nothing to do with them. The point is, they asked for Russia's help. That is very different from being Russian, and so that is why Russia is not in not-Ukraine helping them, and so it has not invaded not-Ukraine.

And anyway, what about Iraq?

## Special Military Operation

A 3-day Special Military Operation is a more recent addition to what definitely isn't an invasion. These are done in response to NATO expansion, which we will see is an unexplainable phenomenon. We will later learn how difficult the past can be for a tankie but for now, you may have noticed that the reasons for the Special Military Operation changed. Initially it was NATO expansion, but this changed over time because the past is an uncertain concept.

It is hard to discuss the Special Military Operation too much because the situation in 2022 remains fluid (especially for Russia's Navy, a large part of which is under a lot of fluid). What can be said is that it appears to involve a lot of feints, goodwill gestures, regroupings, evacuations, and withdrawals to more advantageous positions that are all part of the plan.

Above all, it is not for a tankie to ask why the reason for the Special Military Operation keeps changing (we will address the challenges of the past later). The point is that at any instant all of the reasons for the special military operation can be true, or none of them true, it just depends. Our cause is too noble and virtuous to be constrained by facts anyway.

And anyway, what about Iraq?

## Ceasefires

As further proof that Russia is peaceful and has never invaded anyone, you need only count how many ceasefires Russia is surrounded by.

## Chapter 2: Quiz

1. Russia has never, ever invaded anyone. True/False
2. Entering a country to protect Russians abroad is legitimate. True/False
3. Russia is a peaceful country, surrounded by _____. (Complete)

# Chapter 3.
## What about Iraq?

This is the most important rule. It is important to not argue with imperialists using facts or on the point in question. As we learned in Chapter 1, Russia does not and never has invaded anyone. Therefore, when it can be suggested that it *may* have invaded someone and you, the tankie, don't feel it is right to explain the complexities of *why* Russia has never invaded anyone, distracting your opponent with "what about...?" is a gold-standard tried-and-true strategy.

Now, saying "what about Iraq?" may be seen to imply one of two things about Russia. Firstly, it could be thought to mean that Russia is only *as* bad as the imperialists because it invaded Ukraine or Georgia or Moldova, just as the USA did Iraq. This is a ridiculous notion, as you learned in Chapter 1. This leaves the second option: the idea that because the USA invaded Iraq, which was obviously wrong, it means that Russia invading somewhere is therefore not also wrong. Quite logical, isn't it?

Be aware of both of these in case of a serious mocking, in which case simply keep repeating all the times the USA went to war and hope they don't know how many times Russia didn't invade anyone. Facts have an inherently imperialist bias and logic, as we shall see, is an imperialist construct. In order to defeat the forces of Western colonialism they should be disregarded.

Another point to be aware of is that when the USA invades or bombs somewhere, it is not only wrong and imperialist, but also a humanitarian catastrophe that can be directly related to global instability and terrorism. When Russia invades or bombs a place it is absolutely anti-imperialist but also causes joy amongst the fortunate targets and in no way causes refugees and instability. In short: USA bombing/invading is bad and causes misery, Russia invading/bombing causes joy and unicorns.

Advanced anti-imperialists often remind war-shills that "whataboutism" is a necessary tactic to highlight the crimes of the West. Thus, it is undeniable that logic is an imperialist construct that can be disregarded. Remember this going forward.

## Chapter 3: Quiz

1. Russian bombing causes
   _____. (Complete)
2. Logic is an imperialist _____.
   (Complete)
3. If USA does something wrong, it is not wrong for Russia to do the same wrong. True/False

# Chapter 4.
# The "Near Abroad".

This chapter is an important one and will form the foundation of numerous, important aspects of being a good tankie. The crucial thing to take from this chapter is that countries on or near Russia's borders (the "near abroad") were created to be buffer states between Russia and those Western countries that actually matter, such as France or Germany. This means, logically, that countries fortunate enough to currently share a border with Russia have fewer rights than countries in the West.

In the name of anti-imperialism, these countries need to be neutral and non-aligned, by which we mean a pro-Russian neutrality and a non-aligned status in favor of Russia. In a pro-Russian, non-aligned neutrality, Moscow controls the neutral, nonaligned country's foreign policy as well as who can be in charge of the neutral, nonaligned country. Decisions about who is in charge of Russia's neighbors are too important to be left to the countries in question and are best taken by Moscow. This may sound like imperialism, but it is a necessary aspect of international relations.

It might also sound like realpolitik to an imperialist but that's better than everyone dying in a nuclear holocaust because Kiev got above itself and decided it was an actual country and not a buffer state. We will expand upon this in a later chapter.

What it all amounts to is that these buffer states can't join certain international organizations without Moscow's permission. By "organizations" we mean NATO and, in certain cases like Ukraine, the European Union. Doing so is a direct threat to Russia, which is an entirely peaceful country surrounded by ceasefires – we learned that in Chapter 2.

Chapter 4: Quiz

1. Countries that were created on or near Russia's border were ordained by fate to be buffer states. True/False
2. Does neutrality mean you have to be pro-Russian?
3. Are decisions of who runs a "neutral" country allowed to be taken by that country?

# Chapter 5.
# Protests in the "Near Abroad".

We all know that the 2014 Maidan coup in Ukraine was a CIA plot. It is clear that protesters were given cycling helmets and rolling pins by the CIA before being sent to smash their heads against the batons of heavily armed riot police. Later they were also shot by American snipers in false flag attacks designed to make Russia look bad.

Obviously, Russian intelligence obviously has overwhelming proof of this massive US operation but refuses to release any of it. This is of no concern to us as the last thing we tankies want is widely accepted proof that the USA conducted regime change in Europe, leading to the deaths of over 100 civilians and the ousting of a flawlessly elected democratic President. This would be a disaster for the cause of anti-imperialism and would absolutely not help bring about the removal of the USA and its military bases from Europe as outraged governments across the Continent seek to prevent the same thing happening to them. Evidence, common sense, and logic are tools of the imperialists.

As a tankie you need to be aware that all protests east of Poland and South of Italy (the "near abroad") are CIA operations. These are aimed at overthrowing whichever totally legitimate regime happens to have been in power for years and years, looted the country and left the vast majority in mind-bending poverty. People in these countries cannot protest for themselves without help from the West (by which we mean CIA and maybe MI6). Therefore, protesters in post-Soviet or pro-Russian countries are engaged in an illegal coup and are probably in the pay of Soros. This isn't "west-splaining" or insulting to these people. It is important as a tankie you realize this. Under no circumstances must you be on the side of the poor in this case. Always side with the oligarchic class ruling the country. This is the price of anti-imperialism.

A better way is to describe them as "color revolutions" which are all foreign backed, illegal attempts at constraining Russia by overthrowing the "legitimate government". Euromaidan, the Orange Revolution, and the Rose Revolution, are all good examples. But it's best not to continue this line of thinking too far or you might end up realizing the Bolshevik Revolution that created the glorious paradise of the Soviet Union was also an illegal, foreign-backed color revolution that overthrew the legitimate government. That would be really awkward.

By contrast all protests against governments in Western countries are legitimate public expressions of discontent against out of touch regimes who are also in the pay of Soros. That is because Western people *are* able to protest against their rulers without the CIA or MI6.

Chapter 5: Quiz

1. All protests east of Poland and south of Italy are
   a _____ plot. (Complete)
2. Protesters in former Soviet space are in pay of
   whom?
3. Protests against western leaders are legitimate
   as they are in the pay of whom?

# Chapter 6.
# NATO expansion.

It is a well-known fact that NATO promised Gorbachev it would not expand "one inch east" once Germany was reunified. This promise, which is not written down, is binding. It also overrides any desires the countries in question may have for their own destiny. As we established, these countries have fewer rights than Western countries that were not created to be buffer zones between Russia and Europe and must therefore act accordingly.

You must be aware that the fact Gorbachev's own words on the topic (to a Russian state news outlet) that no such promise was ever made is just further proof that facts have an imperialist bias. It is possibly for this reason that Russia keeps Gorbachev's notes from the time an official state secret. The very last thing the cause of anti-imperialism would need is actual proof of Russia's claims. It is enough that Russia says it is true and therefore you must believe it is true. Facts and evidence are imperialist.

The simple truth is that NATO (by which we mean the US State Department) made a promise to the Soviet Union (by which we mean Russia, but more on that later) that NATO would not move east. To delve deeper into this, NATO promised a country that no longer exists (the USSR) that none of the countries east of Germany, some of which no longer exist (Czechoslovakia, former

Yugoslav Republics) and some which then didn't exist (the Czech Republic, Slovakia, numerous former Yugoslav Republics, the Baltic states) would be allowed to join the alliance. These countries, especially the ones that didn't exist at the end of the Cold War, are bound by this absolutely non-imperialist promise that was made over their heads and without their consent or knowledge, in the name of anti-imperialism. We can all agree that it's really quite clear once you think of it in that way.

There is another point to consider. It remains a genuine mystery why NATO remains so popular amongst Russia's former colonies and neighbors. Who can explain why so many of these countries want to join the alliance? It remains a complete mystery and you, the tankie, must continue to be perplexed by it if asked. You are, of course, more intellectual than your imperialist friends. You can also just say "NATO bombed Serbia!".

Now, this doesn't of course answer the question "Why is NATO so popular?" but it does slow the average imperialist and that must be your goal here. Needless to say, NATO should have done nothing about the Bosnian genocide and allowed it to proceed unchecked. It is a necessary price to pay for anti-imperialism – a lesson that rings true even today, except for when Russia says it must stop a genocide, in which case it's just fine to bomb a place. Anyway, have you ever met a person killed in genocide who didn't think it was worth it to fight NATO colonialism? To sum up, NATO's popularity is an unexplainable conundrum.

Whichever argument you pose, you may be sure it has absolutely nothing to do with anything Russia has done in the past to these countries. Russia is also a peaceful country, surrounded by ceasefires and threatening to defend yourself against Russia is a provocation that Russia has the right to preemptively defend itself against.

## NATO is really weak. Except when it isn't

All good tankies cheered when NATO withdrew from Afghanistan. Compared to the glorious Soviet experience in Afghanistan, NATO's was a complete disaster. The USSR lost four times as many soldiers in half the time as NATO did whilst killing several hundred thousand more civilians before losing to the same people NATO did. It is completely different!

It was naturally a source of delight to all good tankies when a progressive, anti-imperialist group like the Taliban took power in Kabul. This showed that NATO is a weak alliance and not a real military like Russia's. It might be said that this is what happens to a military when it goes "woke", but as tankies are often "woke", too, that's awkward.

The only reason Russia had to make a series of "feints" (not retreats), "goodwill gestures" (not retreats), "re-groupings" (not retreats) and "re-organizations" (not retreats) is because most of the Ukrainian is army is made up of NATO soldiers.

So, you see, my fellow tankie, NATO is *weak* because it lost to Afghanistan but also *amazing* because it beat Russia in Ukraine. On the higher level of tankie thinking this is not a contradiction. It certainly isn't the case that describing an enemy as both strong and weak is a widely regarded aspect of fascism because that would be logical, and we've learned the logic is an imperialist construct.

Chapter 6: Quiz

1. Facts have an _____ bias. (Complete)
2. Threatening to defend yourself against Russia is a _____ (Complete)
3. Who can explain why NATO is so popular amongst countries that currently share a border with Russia?

# Chapter 7.
# The Warsaw Pact.

Transnational, US-led military alliances are a Cold War-era threat to global security kept in being only so western defense contractors can make money. As discussed, their continued popularity amongst countries lucky enough to currently have a border with Russia is a complete mystery. As a good tankie you must never accept that there is a queue to get into NATO, despite imperialist facts to the contrary.

A transnational, Soviet-led military alliance, on the other hand, was a global force for good. So much so that Warsaw Pact members repeatedly attacked themselves before leaving as soon as they could and joining NATO. Fortunately, there are tankies, like you, who have never been to those countries and don't know any of their history, who can "west-splain" to them why they are wrong about NATO and how they have been forced into the alliance against their will.

Recall that at the end of the Cold War millions of people came out to demand that Russian troops not leave their countries. Obviously, they wanted to stay in the Warsaw Pact. In fact, hundreds of them lay underneath Soviet tanks in a desperate attempt to prevent Russia "peacefully leaving its own territory of the Soviet Union".

It is important to realize that in its goal for stable, peaceful relations with its neighbors, Russia rightfully regards a secure international border as one which has Russian soldiers on both sides of it. Should those countries express any desire to prevent Russian soldiers returning, that's just NATO recklessly expanding east into Russia's sphere of influence, thereby increasing the risk of war.

Chapter 7: Quiz

1. Never having been to a former Soviet colony means the tankie is perfectly placed to explain why they have nothing to fear from Russia. True/False
2. The Warsaw Pact was a mutual defense alliance that kept _____. (Complete)

# Chapter 8.
# Respecting Russia.

"All Russia wants is respect!"

"Following the Cold War, the West rubbed Russia's nose in it!"

These points are central to being a tankie and you must remember them. It is therefore worth expanding upon them in detail so you can fulfill your duties as a good tankie.

How does one treat Russia with respect? It's actually rather simple and was explained in Chapter 3, so you may need to re-read it. The way to treat Russia with respect is to treat its buffer-state neighbors with less. These are not actual sovereign countries that matter. As we learned in Chapter 3, these countries who were either lucky enough to be part of the USSR, or to genuinely welcome Soviet occupation during World War Two and then afterwards, were created to serve as buffer states. And buffer states, as we know, do not have the same rights and do not deserve the same respect as proper countries.

The current state of the world is entirely the fault of the USA. By treating buffer states as sovereign countries with the same rights as anyone else, they rubbed Russia's nose in it. Perceptive imperialists may point out how these opinions are shared by many on the far right and actual fascists, but the cause of anti-imperialism finds strange bed fellows. This is a necessary price to pay to defend against American colonialism. And anyway, what about Iraq?

## Chapter 8: Quiz

1. Do countries on Russia's border have the same rights as countries that really matter?
   Yes/No/Of course not
2. By treating the above countries as sovereign, the USA did what to Russia?
3. Can you treat Russia's former colonies with respect AND treat Russia with respect?
   Yes/No/Of course not

# Chapter 9.
# Threatening to defend yourself.

We learned in Chapter 2 that Russia never invades anyone, ever. Should it happen to be the case that the Russian army is massed peacefully on a neighbor's current border in attack formation, any threat by that country to defend itself is, naturally, a destabilizing action aimed at Russia. Such a provocation must be met with a response that may involve the country attacking itself, requiring Russia to, for example, protect its "compatriots abroad". Russia may also respond to a request for help from the "legitimate authorities" within that country that, suddenly, no longer exists.

It really is best to not defend yourself, or even threaten to. Remember that Russia never attacks anyone, ever, and is a peaceful country surrounded by ceasefires. As a tankie it is your duty to remind people that several peaceful Russian armored divisions very close to a smaller country is clearly not a threat anyway. It is instead a time to urge caution and restraint. History teaches us that when Russia positions its army along a neighboring border this is *exactly* when Russia's vastly smaller neighbors tend to suddenly attack either Russia or themselves and force Russia to defend itself in their country. Another point to remember is that while 200,000 Russian troops and their tanks on a border isn't a threat, 400 Canadians and some Humvees in a fake country like Latvia (remember – Buffer State!) is a massive threat and should be condemned at all times.

Other buffer states who may be watching developments in Ukraine need to remember their status in the anti-imperialist world order. This means they must not get any ideas about joining NATO. That would be a threat to stability that runs counter to their status as buffer states.

Chapter 9: Quiz

1. Russia is a peaceful country, surrounded by _____. (Complete)
2. Russia's neighbors always attack Russia when the Red Army is _____ massed in attack formation. (Complete)

# Chapter 10.
## September 1939 to June 1941.

It is vital that as a tankie you realize that absolutely nothing happened between September 1939 & June 1941. From the point where the USSR was forced (repeat *forced*), to sign a deal with the Nazis until it involuntarily switched to the Allied side in June 1941, absolutely nothing happened at all.

In fact, it is fair to say that the West caused World War Two by not aligning with Stalin. His entirely reasonable offer to France and the UK that the Soviet Union occupy all of Poland to prevent fascism should never have been rejected. France and the UK were expected to accept this over the heads of Poland, who were not themselves consulted, but this is irrelevant. Yes, great powers doing deals with other great powers over the heads of small nations may sound like imperialism to some. However, we have already learned that certain countries were created to serve as buffer zones between Russia and other countries that actually matter. Poland is one of those buffer states, so it can't be imperialist to do this.

Neo-colonialists may also point out that Stalin carried out industrial scale mass murder in the half of Poland that he got from Hitler in 1939 after Poland, to everyone's surprise, suddenly and completely ceased to exist. It doesn't follow that the suggestion the Allies give all of Poland to Stalin in a totally non-imperialist way so he could have the whole country in which to commit crimes against humanity would be wrong.  But it also isn't wrong to liberate and protect people from Nazism by killing them.  It also isn't racist to dismiss them because they are Poles. Looking at it like this you can see the West caused World War Two.

Imperialists often suggest that prior to June 1941 the Soviets invaded a string of countries in accordance with a certain secret clause in a certain non-aggression pact Russia was forced to sign.  These facts are imperialist propaganda. Firstly, as a tankie, you need to remember that the Soviets saved these countries from fascism by liberating them from themselves. Never allow imperialists to point out that these so-called countries were driven into a choice between the table manners of cannibals, or between the Black Death and the Red Plague.  Lastly, well-informed imperialists may point out that the USSR admitted the existence of a secret protocol that divided Europe between the USSR and the Nazis.  This was a trick by the CIA to discredit Russia when Russia admitted an awkward fact.

There certainly were no other treaties between the USSR and the Nazis involving economic cooperation, the attempt to end the existence of Poland or any other sensitive issues that could be considered controversial. Dismiss such accusations by reminding imperialists that many countries used to sign non-aggression pacts in those days.  Remember: if imperialists do something wrong then it is not wrong for Russia to do it.  The fact that these other non-aggression pacts didn't have secret clauses to carve up Europe is irrelevant. It also does not matter that the USSR had existing non-aggression pacts at the time with Poland and Finland but preferred the one with Nazis.

The Munich Agreement of 1938 caused World War Two and it is not for anti-imperialists such as we to ask why the USSR didn't inform Hitler that the USSR would declare war should he invade Poland, as France and the UK did. The fact that Russia tries hard to justify doing a deal with Hitler is not relevant. It also does not matter that the West's policy of appeasement has been condemned for decades and none of their governments is currently trying to justify it. We will also learn later that there are times when appeasement is just fine but if in doubt, you can always just say "What about Iraq?".

Chapter 10: Quiz

1. Is it imperialism for the USSR to ask France and the UK to agree to an occupation of Poland without asking Poland?
2. Who tricked the USSR into admitting it had a secret clause in its pact with the Nazis?
3. What happened between September 1939 and June 1941?

# Chapter 11.
# We just don't want a war you neocon shill!

There really is nothing worse than the media pushing for a war, to quote a certain Moscow resident whose tweets are not pre-approved by Russian intelligence. It was CNN that placed 200,000 Russian soldiers on the previous border of Russia and Ukraine, MSNBC who annexed Crimea and the BBC who shot down MH17. Anyone criticizing the benign presence of 200,000 Russian soldiers on Ukraine's border in 2021 was obviously shilling for war. Do they really think that somehow the Kremlin is responsible for putting them there?

To support the above and not get caught out by imperialists in this area, the tankie may need to review several previous chapters. Russia never invades anyone, ever. Therefore, Russian soldiers massed in attack formation can only be a defensive action against a vastly smaller neighbor. Furthermore, threatening to defend yourself against Russia is escalatory and de-stabilizing. Finally, when a buffer state such as Ukraine gets above itself and conducts foreign policy independent of Moscow, this is obviously very threatening and may regrettably require battalions of Russian troops to violently defend themselves inside that buffer state.

However, this chapter was about introducing another argument to your development as a tankie, that of "we don't want a war, you neocon war shill!". The best course of action to reduce international tension may well be to give Russia what it wants. Russia obviously has legitimate security concerns in countries like Ukraine and the Western obsession with containing Russia in Russia is, as we know, imperialist. The West should in this case force Ukraine, or wherever else Russia may be not threatening on a given day, to make reasonable concessions to Russia. It may smack of appeasement for a Westerner to give Russia something of (for example) Ukraine's that is neither theirs to give nor Russia's to take but, as more than one well-known professor may have pointed out, "that's just how the world works". Certainly, it is the way we want the multipolar world will work.

There is no historical parallel we can draw from this, either recently or from 1938. We know that the West caused World War 2 by appeasement, which was wrong, so appeasement now isn't wrong. More recently, we can point to the fact that Russia was appeased over Georgia and Russia then decided to not remove its troops from that buffer state. Russia was appeased over Crimea whose referendum was obviously a flawless democratic event, but the population are entirely pro-Russian anyway. The fact that they may be pro-Russian because the indigenous population were deported and replaced with Russians doesn't matter. Look at the way in which the USA oppresses its native population. That's the elephant in the room.

Russia was also appeased over the parts of Eastern Ukraine it had nothing to do with so, clearly, appeasing Russia now over the entirety of Ukraine is the obvious way out.

The point here that is important is that we tankies are pacifists, that's why we support Russia. Russia never invades anyone. Giving Russia what it wants and allowing it to occupy a country that has ceased to exist because, really, it shouldn't have in the first place, for example Ukraine, is the path to peace. It will save lives and prevent unnecessary deaths, as it did in Katyn in 1940 and in Bucha in 2022. Total indifference to the lives of East Europeans really is for the best. You've never met anyone from those places who didn't mind being murdered in the name of anti-imperialism and neither have your imperialist friends.

A vital thing to understand here is that imperialism isn't some action that a country *does*, it is something a country *is*. The USA in particular but other western European countries too are, by definition, imperialist. Other countries, such as Russia are, existentially, not imperialist, and therefore cannot do imperialist things.

Armed with these facts we tankies may shape our responses accordingly. When an imperialist country does something wrong, we must oppose these actions on moral grounds – "no peace without justice, no justice without truth!" was the rallying cry.

However, when an inherently anti-imperialist country does the same thing, the situation is to be approached on the basis of realpolitik. That's why we suggested Ukraine be reasonable and cede territory in the name of peace to prevent a nuclear war. Yes, their homes got destroyed but people lose their homes in natural disasters, and no one blames Russia for that. Russia is a reasonable country with whom a lasting peace can be achieved if we are just prepared to compromise and give it everything it wants. If Ukraine is carved up, that's a price we have to be willing to let Ukraine pay. This is the path to peace, a path we will most assuredly take, as Russia is a perfectly reasonable negotiating partner who will cause nuclear Armageddon if it doesn't get what it wants.

This realpolitik approach didn't apply to the founding fathers of tankiedom. For example, the people of Vietnam found themselves fighting a vastly bigger, nuclear armed power in the form of the USA. Despite America facing a humiliating defeat and with the potential to lash out and end humanity if its security concerns were not met, we tankies adopted a purely moral approach to the situation. Arming North Vietnam did not escalate and prolong the war, cause unnecessary suffering or further a proxy war against the USA. That only applies when a place like Ukraine is under attack. Arming buffer states so they can protect themselves only makes things worse for them. This approach only applies when dealing with an imperialist power like the USA and certainly not to Ukraine or anyone else under attack by imperialist clients of the USA.

Remember, certain western countries are inherently imperialist whereas Russia is inherently anti-imperialist. The actions of each therefore require either moral or realpolitik approaches. US tanks in a place they aren't invited to is bad. Russian tanks in a place they aren't invited to is good. Hence: tankie.

## Chapter 11: Quiz

1. Are Russia's troops massed in attack formation on a neighboring country's current border a threat?
2. Is containing Russia to within Russia's own borders imperialist?
3. Does appeasement always work?

# Chapter 12.
# The Past Changes Quickly.

February 2022 was a challenging time to be a tankie. For months many of us had confidently and loudly assured everyone that firstly, there were no Russian tanks on Ukraine's borders and that it was just "the media pushing for war". Then, secondly, it turned out there were in fact quite a lot of tanks and they were indeed right on Ukraine's border. It was, of course, hysterical to suggest they were threatening anyone. They were in Russia and that's all that matters.

Then it turned out that US intelligence was right all along. How awkward was that?

This brings us to an important aspect of anti-imperialism: the past can change very quickly. So quickly that sometimes we cannot predict what will happen yesterday. You might think that having been so categorically and, in many cases, volubly and spectacularly wrong about Russia's plans to invade Ukraine, that it would be wise, perhaps even moral, for a tankie to, well, shut up.

Luckily, you don't need to remember how wrong you were because the past is so uncertain. Of course, the war was not going to happen at all, but then it did. That means that it was the fault of NATO expansion and Ukraine wanting to become a hostile state on its current border with Russia. Sadly, it can be hard to make imperialists believe that NATO has made Russia bomb hospitals, schools and power stations while killing loads of civilians. This means that instead of the war being because of NATO, it was because there were secret biolabs making a strain of COVID that can only infect Russians. But anyway, the past changed so quickly that we cannot be certain what happened yesterday, and it may change again tomorrow.

You must remain firm in your anti-imperialist beliefs and principles, despite the existence of imperialist facts to the contrary. Do not allow your being wrong about the war even to *starting* prevent you from explaining why it actually did: NATO expansion! Biolabs! Weaponized Bats! Satanism!

Chapter 12: Quiz

1. The past changes so quickly that you have no idea what will happen _____. (When?)
2. The fact that you, as a tankie, were wrong about the invasion happening means you are perfectly placed to explain why it actually happened. True/False
3. The fact that you, as a tankie, were wrong about the invasion happening means you are perfectly placed to explain how to stop it. True/False

# Chapter 13.
# The Lamestream Media.

Good tankies avoid mainstream media - especially state funded media such as the BBC and CNN - at all costs. A superior source of information is Russian state-funded media as it has no editorial independence and a massive budget.

You might be questioned about the credibility of Russian state media as a reliable news source, perhaps because it has occasionally fabricated stories about crucified babies or published doctored pictures of refugees in ways that are absolutely not racist. However, "Truth" is a myth. When the "lamestream media" broadcast a geo-located photograph of a Russian tank (of a type only Russia has) parked in front of a daycare center in Donetsk, but Kremlin-controlled media reports that not only was it never there, but it isn't even a tank, who are you supposed to believe? The answer should be obvious.

It can also be stressed by a wise tankie that news organizations like the BBC are *basically* the same as Kremlin-controlled media anyway. Imperialists may point out that the BBC had a very public fight over the lies that led to the Iraq war and the so-called "dodgy dossier" and that no Russian state media would ever do that to the Kremlin. This is clearly a trick to get you to imagine, for example, the editor of a Kremlin media outlet getting into a public argument about Russian invasions without winding up face-down outside the Kremlin having shot himself in the back four times.

It is true that the Western lamestream media accurately predicting the Russian invasion of Ukraine can lead to some awkward conversations.  But what about Iraq?

Chapter 13: Quiz

1. Are western state-funded media (that do have editorial independence) "mainstream media"?
2. Are Russian state-funded media (that does not have editorial independence) "mainstream media"?
3. What would happen to a journalist in Russia if they claimed Russia was manufacturing consent for an invasion?

# Chapter 14.
# In Ukraine, Russia is only doing what great powers do.

After weeks of scoffing at the very notion of Russia invading Ukraine, many experienced tankies were caught by surprise when Russia seemed to invade Ukraine. Early signs were dismissed because they came from the USA, best known for saying that Iraq had WMD and being imperialist. Annoyingly, when Russia did seem to actually invade, it appeared to tankies who were not one-hundred-percent loyal that when US intelligence isn't massaged by idiots it can be quite effective. There was, for a short time, cause for concern because US intelligence had been exactly right.

At least that's what an imperialist would say, as Russia seemed to invade Ukraine. Tankies who knew their anti-imperialist rhetoric well quickly remembered that Russia was just defending itself inside another country and that it isn't wrong for them to do so because the USA also did that somewhere. Russia of course cannot allow Ukraine to become a NATO stronghold right on its border. We already know that it is a complete mystery why so many of Russia's neighbors want to join NATO, so Ukraine's desire to join can only be a CIA plot to break apart Russia. This is foundational tankie lore.

A loyal tankie may point out: "The USA disallowed hostile bases in Cuba, and also tried to invade it, so you can't complain about Russia not allowing hostile bases in Ukraine by actually invading it". Of course, everyone knows that NATO wanted to do this in Ukraine, that's why it refused to let Ukraine join the alliance. Everyone also knows that US behavior towards Cuba is imperialist and wrong, which means Russia acting in the same way is therefore not also wrong. Simple.

By now you are beginning to appreciate how the foundational dogma of being a tankie supports all aspects of our morally superior world view.

## If a US neighbor joined a hostile alliance?

Having established that Russia isn't wrong for doing the same wrong thing the USA did, we can now pose the question "Well, what would the USA do if Mexico or Canada joined a military alliance with Russia and allowed Russian bases to be stationed on the US border?". You can forgive yourself for feeling smug at this point as you watch your imperialist squirm. This is evidence of their attempting to reconcile your inarguable logic with their flawed worldview and should not be construed as disgust or pity. They may point out that neither Mexico nor Canada feels any need for external military protection from the USA, so why do so many of Russia's neighbors feel the need for protection from Moscow? A child's argument. The fact that the USA shares the world's longest undefended border with Canada is merely proof that one day Ottawa will realize how close they are to being invaded and immediately seek an alliance with Moscow.

It is important to note that there is no way Russia could have removed any need to use its military by just being a better option to its neighbors than NATO is. It certainly cannot be suggested that the reason neither Canada nor Mexico seek military protection from the USA because it is, axiomatically, a better partner than a military alliance with Moscow or Beijing would provide. That would be logical, and logic can be dismissed if it's the choice between that and anti-imperialism. Checkmate.

Chapter 14: Quiz

1.  Do tankies have to explain why neighbors to the USA do not feel need for military protection from the USA?
2.  Is it ok for Russia to treat Ukraine the same way the USA treats Cuba?
3.  Should Russia just be a better option to its neighbors than NATO is?

# Chapter 15.
# Everyone wants to overthrow the Kremlin.

As we learned in Chapter 1, the West is engaged in a sustained effort at regime change in Russia for reasons that make perfect sense to you, the tankie, but sound like lunacy to imperialists led astray by their common sense, evidence, and facts. This means that all opposition to the Kremlin is a CIA front, as we have already learned. Since we know what the CIA is doing and who they are doing it with, let us now learn how they do it.

Imagine a certain high profile Russian opposition figure who is in Russia and under the close surveillance of Russian intelligence because he is a CIA asset. He leaves a hotel in Russia to go to an airport in Russia where he will fly from Russia to Russia. During his flight he is poisoned by a Russian nerve agent only Russia has and slips into a coma. This is obviously one of three things. One, it is a CIA operation to get him to the West where he can receive further orders for his regime change mission by being outside Russia in a coma and nearly dead. Two, it is a false flag assassination to discredit Russia whereby regime change is achieved by having all plausible alternative leaders of Russia dead. Or three, it may in fact be both at the same time, regardless of the fact that they appear mutually exclusive.

As a tankie, you need to be able to think on a higher level than normal people and believe logically incompatible things simultaneously. We must also disregard the implication that Russian intelligence is too incompetent to prevent this massively complex operation.

It all makes perfect, rational sense, doesn't it?

Chapter 15: Quiz

1. Is the CIA trying to carry out regime change in Russia by killing members of the Russian opposition?
2. Is the CIA also trying to carry our regime change in Russia by removing members of the Russia opposition from Russia?
3. Can you believe these two incompatible statements at the same time?

# Chapter 16.
# Russia is concerned by the rise of the far right in the West.

Russia, which has never allied with any far-right organization in history, but also frequently invites the far right to the Kremlin, onto state-controlled media and provides loans to them from Russian-controlled banks, is deeply concerned by the far right in the West. The fact that various members of the far-right in the West all really like the Kremlin is not relevant. Be they from France, Italy, Holland, the UK, the USA or wherever, Russia remains the only country willing to stand up to these far-right groups who like the Kremlin so much. Any pictures you may see of far-right figures having meetings with the Kremlin at the Kremlin posted by the Kremlin are CIA propaganda.

It is important to understand the need to be consistent about politicians expressing far right views. If certain prominent Russian opposition politicians, who are absolutely CIA operatives, have in the past expressed far-right views, that's proof of the rise of Fascism in the West. If a French presidential candidate or potential Italian PM who really likes the Kremlin says the exact same thing that's no cause for concern. Just remember, if someone who opposes the Kremlin has far right views, it's proof that only Putin can save Europe from the abyss of Nazism.

Chapter 16: Quiz

1. Does it matter to you, the tankie, that almost all of the West's far right all like the Kremlin?
2. Russian opposition politician says far right things. (Good/bad?)
3. Western politician who is pro Russia says far right things. (Good/bad?)

# Chapter 17.
# The successor state to the USSR.
# Except when it isn't.

Imperialists enjoy pointing out that the USSR committed many and various crimes against humanity. Some of these happened before the USSR was forced to switch to the Allied side in 1941. Awkwardly, some of these were committed after the end of World War Two as well, against people who had already "been liberated from fascism" but also needed to be liberated from themselves and from breathing. We will discuss how the USSR won World War Two all by itself. By extension this means Russia won World War Two all by itself, remembering of course that we learned earlier that nothing happened before Russia switched sides, and also that Ukrainians and Belarusians fighting the Nazis don't count. This means the Russia is the USSR when it's good to be and it isn't when it isn't, such as when tens of thousands of people are being murdered.

Therefore, Russia both is, and is not, the Soviet Union. Knowing when it is and when it is not will help you defeat the combined forces of imperialist logic and facts. Think of it as the "Union of Schrodinger's Soviet Republics"

Chapter 17: Quiz

1. It can be thought of as the Union of
   _____ Soviet Republics. (Complete)
2. Who won World War Two all by itself?
3. Therefore, did Russia win World War Two all by
   itself?

# Chapter 18.
# Conclusion

Congratulations on reaching the end of this book. By now you should be much better equipped to out-debate your imperialist opponent with their facts, evidence, logic, and reason. Our cause is too noble to be constrained by such considerations. Once you have passed the test below and can call yourself a loyal tankie, you can go forth and spread the word while humiliating imperialists, colonialists, and war shills. Just remember, that if you can't make an imperialist believe one thing, you can always try to make them believe nothing. Then they will do nothing as the armies of anti-imperialism advance, sometimes in reverse, towards the multi-polar world.

That is true master strategy.

# Chapter 19.
# Quiz Answers.

## Chapter 1 Russia is just defending itself
1. True
2. No
3. True

## Chapter 2 Russia never invaded anyone
1. True
2. True
3. Ceasefires

## Chapter 3 What about? What about? What about?
1. Joy and unicorns
2. Construct
3. True

## Chapter 4 The "Near Abroad"
1. True
2. Yes
3. No

## Chapter 5 Protests in the "Near Abroad"
1. CIA
2. Soros
3. Soros

## Chapter 6 NATO expansion
1. Imperialist
2. Provocation or threatening to Russia
3. No one can

Chapter 7 The Warsaw Pact
1. True
2. Attacking itself

Chapter 8 Respecting Russia
1. Of course not
2. Humiliate
3. Of course not

Chapter 9 Threatening to defend yourself
1. No
2. CIA
3. Absolutely nothing

Chapter 10 September 1939 to June 1940
1. No
2. CIA
3. Absolutely nothing

Chapter 11 We just don't want a war you neo-con shill!
1. No
2. Yes
3. Trick question. It depends if it's Russia being appeased.

Chapter 12 The Past Changes Quickly
1. Yesterday
2. True
3. True

Chapter 13 The Lamestream Media
1. Yes
2. No

3. Multiple self-inflicted gunshots to the back (or similar)

Chapter 14 In Ukraine, Russia is only doing what great powers do
1. No
2. Yes
3. No

Chapter 15 Everyone wants to overthrow the Kremlin
1. Yes
2. Yes
3. Yes

Chapter 16 Russia is concerned by the far right
1. No
2. Bad
3. Good

Chapter 17 The successor state to the USSR. Except when it isn't
1. Schrodinger's
2. USSR
3. Yes

Number correct _____ / 50

# Chapter 21.
# What level of tankie are you?

Congratulations on completing the book and the test! Knowing your final score, you can now grade yourself as to what level of tankie you are.

Less than 18 correct – Level achieved: "Imperialist lickspittle". You got at least two thirds of the questions wrong! This is a sign of an imperialist lickspittle in the pay of CIA and Soros. You are quite likely a warmonger and a neocon shill who wants to destroy Russia and trigger nuclear war. Read the book again!

Between 18 and 27 correct. Level achieved: "Imperialist Warmonger". You still got less than half correct. A steady diet of Kremlin controlled news and re-reading this book may help you. Serious concerns remain. You are being watched.

Between 28 and 40 correct. Level Achieved: "Tankie Traitor". You got over, or well over half correct. You might think you have solid, anti-imperialist potential and credentials but actually you are most likely a traitor to our noble cause. Perhaps you think that Russian soldiers being in another country shooting things is wrong, just as it was when US soldiers were doing that. This indicates treason to the near sacred cause of anti-imperialism. This is worse than the two lower levels and you should be canceled.

Between 40 and 46 correct:  Level Achieved: "Solid Tankie".  You got over 75% right.  Perhaps you wavered over recent events in Ukraine but have stayed mostly loyal and are not a lost cause.  Perhaps some extra reading of the required literature will remove these potential biases of logic.

Over 47 correct:  Level Achieved: "Supreme, professor emeritus of tankie".  You are on the side of right on every single issue and no one can question your commitment, ethics, or consistency.  You recognize the imperialist nature of facts, logic, and evidence.  You may look at your warmongering associates with smug condescension and hope that one day they will look past the evidence of their eyes and ears and see the true light.  Well done.

# Author's note

Many people helped to make this book possible and encouraged me to write it.  They all have my thanks.  The idea for this book grew out of a thread of tweets called "How to Tankie: The Darth Putin Guide" posted in January 2022.  As a thread it did fairly well in terms of retweets but a lot of people who've written books on Russia and International Relations were very complimentary.  Some of them said "this could be a book" and I eventually I came to agree and overcame my reluctance to write it.  The thread allowed for cut & paste replies to the talking points trolls & tankies come up with that appeared in Darth's timeline. They only ever make the same points - "NATO expansion", "Nazis in Kiev", "What about Iraq?" and so on, without considering the points raised in this book.  I hope that by putting it all together as I have done here, I can help make your social media experience better.

I also think it is mostly a waste of time to argue with trolls and tankies.  They not only have their own opinions but also their own facts (facts which seemed to change on an hourly basis in early 2022).  However, lots of people argue with them and I generally see two types of people who do it.  Firstly, those who are prepared to tie themselves in knots and spend ages arguing with these accounts as if they can win some kind of reasoned debate.  This gives the troll or tankie the credit of having an argument with some merit and this is almost never the case.  Secondly, those who just get really mad, often at an inauthentic account trying to cause division, thinking they can somehow out-anger them.

Each group seems to think they will get the last word or somehow come up with a "gotcha" tweet that will shut them up. Both are pointless in my view as reason and facts are irrelevant to them and there is no "gotcha" post you can make to "win".

Being Darth comes fairly easy and I don't spend as much time doing it as you might think, mostly because the satire largely writes itself but also trolls and tankies make the same arguments and tell the same lies over and over. Once you know how to deal with them, as often as not, the trolls will block you, not the other way around - at least that's what many Russian embassies, diplomats, media employees and very active trolls have done to Darth after being mocked. Ever since I created Darth, I've watched people debate with trolls and tankies as if the arguments those accounts put forward actually have merit instead of just being absurd. That is exactly what they crave - to be taken seriously by the "establishment" they claim to hate. What they truly dislike and can't deal with is to be seen as figures worthy of nothing more than mockery and contempt. That's why I (and a lot of the world's reputable press) believe the Kremlin tried to have Darth banned in 2016. It's also why I wrote this book, to try to persuade you that mockery is a great way to handle it. The current situation isn't funny at all, only a psychopath would think it is. That doesn't mean we have to pretend the people excusing it and denying crimes against humanity committed in plain view are above being mocked for peddling lies and absurdities.

Darth Putin KGB. October 2022.